T0039245

My Mama Sara Bird

Eugenia Crenshaw

authorHOUSE®

AuthorHouse™
1663 Liberty Drive
Bloomington, IN 47403
www.authorhouse.com
Phone: 1 (800) 839-8640

Published by AuthorHouse 05/16/2016

ISBN: 978-1-5049-1405-5 (sc)
ISBN: 978-1-5246-0899-6 (e)

Print information available on the last page.

To those who have been denied the freedom of learning

Dedicated to my mom... one of the strongest women I personally know, and my strongest supporter

To my parents...thank you for giving me and my siblings an awesome childhood!!! (we had fun)

To my sisters and brothers...thank you for putting up with my "sometimes unusual ways"

To Kenyatta "baby girl" Judd for the poem

To Dondra' Howard, thanks for helping with the logo designs so many years ago

The love and protection of a family can last a lifetime. For Sarah, her love would be tried and tested. She would suffer a stepfather whose physical and emotional abuse of her beloved mother would bring her to the edge. Sarah desired to attend school and to protect her mother, both of which were in the forefront of her thoughts. Take a short journey into betrayal, fear, and the spirit of letting go. You will find the simple things in life are very precious and forgiving is a simple decision.

More than thirty-six million adults in America struggle to read according to the National Coalition for Literacy. Please visit the National Coalition for Literacy website at national-coalition-literacy.org for more information.

Chapter 1

I just finished a double shift at the mill, and I attempted to hurry to the car. But I was just too tired to rush. I looked at my watch and realized that I had about an hour to make the thirty-mile drive home and see the children off to school. Then I'd get into bed for a few hours of sleep, fix dinner, and start all over again. I hadn't realized how truly tired I was until I was midway through the drive home. I began to relax, and the road seemed as if it was hypnotizing me into a soft, gentle sleep. When I got home, all five of the children were all dressed and ready for school. My two teenagers were fussing over the usual spot in the bathroom. My two oldest daughters were out of the house. One was married, and the other was away in college. Everyone had a story to tell me as I tried to listen and comprehend all they were saying because they all were talking at the same time. My husband was already gone to work, and my youngest child was still in bed sleeping. *Good,* I thought. *Maybe I can get a few hours of sleep before she wakes and wants breakfast*. The bus finally arrived, and the children rushed out the door. I hurried to the bathroom to take a quick bath, washing all of the cotton remains off from the textile mill. I eased into bed and began to drift into a peaceful sleep when a sharp pain ripped at my chest and ran along my side. I lay in bed, frozen. I couldn't move, and the pain only got worse. *Am I having a stroke?* I couldn't speak, and it would have not done any good because there was no one home but me and my baby. I looked up, and all I thought was, *Lord, help me live to raise my babies*. I closed my eyes and felt the pain ease away and a sudden peace take over. I thought of my mama and all that happened to me that led me to this day as a wife and a mama of eight children. I had come a long way, and I have a long way to travel with my family. Then I saw my past and present in what seemed to be encased in time. *Lord, help me. I don't want anyone else raising my children. They need me, Lord. Save me and keep me alive.* I closed my eyes, knowing that he had answered my prayer, and off I drifted into the things that I had not thought of in many years.

I sat there, rocking and looking. I looked down that long dirt road. I was looking for my papa. I knew that he would be coming to get me any day now. If I would sit and rock, he would certainly come back home, and we would be a family. For the first time we would be a regular family. I would have a papa just like the rest of the children who lived on that dirt road nestled in the woods. When I was school age, I left the rocking chair and replaced it by sitting at the window and watching the children. Most of them were my friends walking to school. I was sitting at that window, wishing that I was walking to school with all of them. Then I heard the rustling and crying behind me. It was the children, and they were up for the day. This was the sixth year of looking out of that window. In 1938, I was six, and most of my friends started school, which was the beginning of my longing to learn. Mama wouldn't let me or my brothers go to school. She was scared that someone would hurt us on the long walk to school. Mama was very protective of us, and since she left for work so early in the morning, she felt that keeping us in the house was the best way to keep us from harm. There was a reason for Mama being so concerned for us, and in no way do I hate her for my not getting an education.

Mama was an only child, and her parents had died when she was very young. She was raised by her elderly grandparents, and when they passed away only several months apart, Mama was on her own at age eighteen. Mama had to provide for herself, and her once happy and sheltered home with her grandparents was over. She left Newberry, South Carolina, and moved to Augusta, Georgia, where she worked as a maid cooking and cleaning for various employers. Leaving home for the first time must have been a fearful event in her life. Mama had no other family left except a cousin. She spent years trying to locate him, but she was never successful. Her family had died out, and she had no knowledge of any other living family members. Augusta, Georgia, was where she met my papa, and he too was from South Carolina. He had grown up in Barnwell County. They married, but the marriage was troubled from the very beginning. My papa liked to drink, and he drank a lot. They moved back to South Carolina near his relatives, but the two of them finally separated for good after years of his excessive drinking. He would leave the family for months at a time, and he was extremely unreliable. Together, they had six children, but now there were three of us, me and my two older brothers, Luther and Charles. Luther was the oldest. Then came Charles, and finally, there was me. I had three older siblings who were older than Luther, but two had died a few years back from the fever. James and Sis was what I thought Mama had called them. I don't remember them, only Elizabeth. I remember Elizabeth holding me and tucking me into bed at night and giving me a lot of love and attention. I remember her lying in bed as she was slowly dying from anemia. Her life lingered for days until she finally slipped away at the age of eighteen. Sadness fell on our house, and a lonely feeling entered my heart that day. Now it was just the three of us children and Mama. My papa was gone before I was born, so I didn't know him at all. All that I knew and always felt was that our lives might have been easier if he was there and I could go to school. Then Mama wouldn't have to work so hard. My mama was called Ruth, and she was an educated woman. She didn't like her birth name, Martha, and she changed it when she became an adult. Her loving grandparents sent her to school. Mama said that she finished all of her schooling, but I am not sure where she attended school.

Mama would read to us when she got home from a long day of work, and she always promised that she would teach us how to read one day. Mama was the sole provider for the house, and she worked hard. But she would take time to read us stories about the potbelly people and things that were happening in the world. The house that we lived in was rented, and Mama had a garden in the back. We grew most of our food. In the summer all the ladies and children would go out into the woods to pick wild blackberries, plumbs, apples, and peaches. Mama would make homemade wine from the blackberries. Mama was a great cook, and she canned everything that she could. We always had food for the winter in the pantry. Although Papa was gone, we continued to live near his relatives. We would all meet at church, and they would sometimes come for dinner. They all loved my mama's cooking, especially my papa's sister, Aunt Janie. She would always say that Mama could make anything taste like honey. Mama was also a great housekeeper. She kept our house clean, and there were always clean and crisp sheets on the beds. Mama and I would get on our knees and scrub the floors, and the house would smell fresh with soap in the air. We lived in the country, and we had a running spring. We would get our water from it to wash our clothes and cook. There was always a lot of work to be done, but we had lots of fun playing too. My brothers and I would go play in the sawdust piles in the woods. I tried and could often keep up with the two of them most of the time. We were always on some sort of adventure. When I was alone, I would dream of being a spy with a long trench coat. Maybe I would work for the government or solve difficult mysteries one day. Our days were full of work and fun, and in the evenings we had stories read to us from one of the books Mama had bought for us. I would listen to every word Mama read and often wished I could read those books for myself. Other than wanting to go to school, I believed that the four of us were doing fine, but one day that all changed. Mama started seeing a man by the name of Sam Turner. Then the peace and protection that we as a family once knew began to change.

Chapter 2

Family Changes

The year I turned ten, Mama married Sam Turner. Mama was a maid, but the two met at the cotton mill where Mama worked to make extra money. Sam was a small man in height and weight, and he was always going to Florida. He would always bring us something back from his trips. Sam would bring us candy and little oranges. I remember being so amazed at the size of those small oranges and how sweet they were. I had never seen anything like them before. Things were fine for the first couple of months, but then Sam changed. The special gifts and the trips to Florida became more and more scarce, and Mama didn't smile as much as she used to. She would sit in her chair, holding her hands as if she was worried about something. Sometimes Mama would go outside to cry. She never said anything to me or my brothers about it. I loved Mama, and I knew something was not right. That's when I began watching her every move. I became that spy I dreamed of becoming, and I was determined to find out what was upsetting Mama. One day I followed her out to the barn. I didn't see anything, but I could hear arguing and then noises that sounded like someone was being hit. As I hid behind the barn, I could see Mama running out of the barn, crying. The problem was Sam, and he was hitting my mama. I don't know what the arguing was about, but Sam was very angry. And his fists were taking it out on my mama. This went on for several weeks. Sam would ask Mama to go to the barn to help him with something, and then he would beat on her for whatever was making him mad. Mama never said anything to us about it. But I had had enough, and I told my brothers Charles and Luther. From that day on, the three of us watched for any signs of trouble, and I watched Mama with a protective eye. A few months had passed since an incident had occurred. Then it finally happened again. Sam asked Mama to help him in the barn, and I followed close behind and stopped short of opening the door when I heard Sam yelling and hitting her. Mama ran out of the barn, crying, and I ran to get Charles and Luther. “What’s wrong with Mama?” Charles shouted.

“It’s Sam, and he’s hitting Mama again,” I screamed. When we got to the barn, Sam was still there. He was pacing around like a caged tiger. Luther, the oldest at seventeen, took quick control over the situation and grabbed Sam by the collar of his shirt. Charles began biting him on the leg, and I began sticking him with the pin that held up my bloomers.

“If you ever touch my mama again,” Luther yelled,” I’ll kill ya.”

“Get away from me, you bastards. You ain’t my children anyway,” was all that Sam could think of saying as he ripped himself from Luther’s grip and stomped out of the barn. The three of us made our point to Sam loud and clear that day, and he knew that hitting our mama was not allowed.

We only had the four of us, and we were going to protect one another no matter what. Luther was serious about killing Sam if he ever hit Mama again. Sam ran straight into the house and shouted at Mama that *her* children had attacked him in the barn. From that time on, Mama avoided going into the barn with Sam because she knew Luther would make good on his promise to kill Sam if he ever hit her again. I later thought about what Sam had called me and my brothers. Sam called us bastards. We were not his children, not that we wanted to be, but I wished that my own papa was there and not Sam Turner. A year had gone by, and Mama was pregnant. Sam and Mama had three children together, and it became my responsibility to take care of them. Once again there was another reason I couldn't go to school. As the years passed, I was still sitting at the window, watching all my friends walk to school, and I was home taking care of Mama and Sam's children. As if Mama needed more problems in her life, my papa's baby sister, Aunt Katherine, moved in one summer. Aunt Katherine had come to stay with us because she had no place to go after her parents, my grandparents, died. None of her brothers or sisters wanted her around. No one would take her into their home. Mama was always kind and giving. She opened our home to Aunt Katherine, although Mama was divorced from her brother. At the very beginning, Katherine was trouble. She was never nice to me, and soon she and Sam had started a relationship that was not appropriate.

When Katherine and Sam wanted to be alone while Mama was working, they would lock me in the closet. I knew they did not want me to tell Mama, and I often cried about it. I did not want to hurt Mama, and I was scared of what Aunt Katherine and Sam would do to me or Mama if I told. They both had threatened me not to say anything. Finally, I'd had enough, and through the tears I told Mama the whole truth. Aunt Katherine had lived with us for about two and a half years. During this time she had given birth to two children. Both were boys, but the first baby had died at birth. No one knew who the father of the children was. Aunt Katherine was not seeing anyone in particular, and she rarely left the house except to shop. When I told Mama that Sam and Katherine locked me in the closet when she was at work, it became obvious to Mama that Sam was the father of Aunt Katherine's children. I'm not sure what Mama said to Katherine or Sam, but I remember that Mama and I walked Aunt Katherine and her baby to the bus stop and left them there. I never saw Katherine again, and we never mentioned her name. Katherine was gone, but Sam remained in our home, slowly breaking Mama's spirit and causing unrest in the house. I wished Sam and Katherine would have left together.

The New Siblings

"The Turner children" is what I called them. They were Mama and Sam's children. The firstborn was Cilia. Then there was Craig and Cissy. Sam couldn't read, and he liked the "S" sound in his daughter's names like his. But Mama spelled their names with the letter "C". Whenever Luther, Charles, and I did something wrong, Mama would discipline us for it, but Mama was not allowed to discipline Sam's children. Sam would often yell at Mama, "Don't touch my children!" He thought the world of them, and they grew up wild and undisciplined. They destroyed everything that they could put their hands on. I was stuck keeping them all day long in the house. They destroyed pictures, my precious tea set that Mama had bought for me, and my beautiful doll babies that were past Christmas gifts. I was tired most days because I had three small children to look after, and I was still a child myself. I cooked, cleaned, and did the housework. How I longed to go to school. I had nice clothes to wear because Mama would make some of my dresses out of flour sacks. Some flour sacks from the 1930s and early 1940s were made out of cloth with beautiful prints on them. My dresses may have been made from sacks, but Mama could make anything look nice. She was very gifted. Mama could make plain things look simply beautiful. These simple gifts made me feel special. I had clothes to wear to school now. I wanted to go so bad, and I became determined to go.

One day our neighbor Mrs. Jean offered her services to help me finally go to school. She would see me at the window, staring at the children going to school, and she offered to watch my siblings while I went to school. I started school in the middle of the school year, but Mrs. Ames, the schoolteacher, along with my friends helped me learn the basics. I was learning the alphabet and their sounds. Every day I was excited to learn some new letter, and I was learning fast. At the beginning I was scared I would not be as smart as the other children because they had been going to school longer than I had. Mrs. Ames took me under her guidance, and the world of learning was opening for me in leaps and bounds until that unfortunate day. Mama got sick at work and came home early. She found the house empty and the chores unfinished. She began to panic and ran from house to house and found the children at Mrs. Jean's house. Mama was really upset with Mrs. Jean and me, and that was the end of my formal education. "Sarah, I want you home taking care of these children. I'll teach you how to read!"

Yeah, one day, I thought sadly to myself. Mama was always making that promise to me and my brothers, but it never happened. Luther and Charles had given up on their dreams of reading, and they were always on some adventure with some of the other boys who didn't go to school. Mama finally allowed Charles to go to school one year, but by then he was too old and impatient and proud to start with what he called "little baby words."

Mama worked such long hours. Her life with Sam wasn't easy. I believe she just did not have the time or the energy to teach me or my brothers how to read. Also, the local authorities of my town did not question parents who did not send their children to school. Many children slipped through the cracks of not getting an education during my childhood. I know of children who had to help on the farms, and some parents did not think it was important. This happened in both black and white families. Charles and Luther had lost all interest in school, but I began to dream that someday when I was older I would learn how to read and write. My friends taught me how to write my name, and I would practice it over and over again. All day I would write and say S-A-R-A-H. No one could take that from me, not Sam, not Mama, and not the Turner children. I could spell my name, and that made me feel smart and independent. Mama heard me spelling my name one day. She was worried about me because I had become so withdrawn from everyone. She saw how sad I was about being taken out of school. Mama tried her best to cheer me up, but nothing worked until she brought Molly home.

Chapter 3

Some Relief

Molly was the best thing that happened to me since I had started school and learned how to spell my name. Molly was a beautiful horse. She was a tall and strong horse, and she was pregnant. She delivered her colt three days after Mama bought her. Mama had planned to use Molly for plowing, but she was given to me to ride. "You can have Molly, but I might have to use her for work sometimes," Mama said. When Mama got home from work and all my chores were done, I would ride that horse for hours with my thick, long hair flying in the wind as Molly galloped through the fields. I felt so peaceful and confident when I was riding Molly. I would forget about the cares of what was going on in our little house. The thoughts of Sam and his unruly children would drift away when I was riding Molly.

Several months had gone by, and Molly was the best companion and distraction for me. I really needed her at that time in my life. That year Charles and Luther had moved out of the house, and now it was just me and the Turner children. Charles had run away, and no one knew where he had gone. He just left one day without saying good-bye. Luther had married his sweetheart, and the two were moving around a lot. Since Charles and Luther had moved out, Sam became bolder with his assaults on Mama. One day I came home from riding Molly, and Mama looked as if she had been crying. She refused to talk about it, and those old feelings of fear and sadness came rushing back to my memory. Sam also began to drink, and some of his drunken friends began hanging around the house. The scent of corn whiskey and stale cigarettes were always on their clothes. Their eyes were always glossy and bloodshot. They were always cussing and whispering among themselves. I stayed away from them, but my younger sisters and brother seemed to enjoy their company. They would sit at the window and listen to all the cussing and storytelling those old bums spewed out on the porch. Soon the Turner children had picked up the same cussing and brawling ways as Sam and his friends. Sam never kept a job. He just floated between working with his friends and doing small odd jobs. He never kept anything of worth. I believe this was one of the problems between him and Mama. As soon as Mama made any money, Sam was there to spend it on one of his good ideas.

Mama got a good job working at the new crate mill that had just opened in town. She put in a good word for Sam and helped him get a job there. Mama was a hard worker, and the owner praised her work. Sam was proud of his new job, and he and Mama received good pay. But Sam's old car was not reliable, and they both almost lost their jobs because they couldn't get to work some days because the car would not start. Luther had moved back to town and had also gotten a job at the crate mill. Luther would pick up Mama and Sam, and they would ride to work together. Sam was nicer to Mama during this time because they both were bringing home steady money, but then Sam's friends began to tease him about being an honest homebody. Sam began to drink more, and he would drink his whiskey before going to work. To prove to himself that he wasn't henpecked, he started beating Mama again. One day in a drunken rage, he started hitting Mama in the kitchen because she wouldn't give him her pay. I ran to my cousin John, and John found Luther.

Luther arrived at the house with his gun and the intention to kill Sam. Luther grabbed Sam's arm as it was coming down on Mama. He pushed Sam to the floor and put the gun to Sam's head. The Turner children were screaming at Luther to let their daddy go. "I told you, Sam, if you ever hit Mama again, I'd kill you," Luther shouted. Mama staggered to her feet and begged Luther not to make good on his promise. Luther saw the fear in Mama's eyes and lowered the gun. Sam began to cuss, but that was all he could do. Sam looked scared.

"Sam, I think you'd better leave," Mama said sadly.

"I'm glad to leave!" Sam hissed with hate in his eyes as he looked at me, Luther, and Mama. "Y'all ain't 'nothing anyways."

The Turner children went running after their daddy, crying, "We want to go with you, Daddy!" Sam left the house, but Mama let him come back the next day. After that incident Sam was not about to ride to work with Luther.

Sam struck up a deal with one of the foremen at the job. He traded Molly's colt for a car. He didn't tell Mama what he had planned to do. The man just showed up with his daughter, and they took the colt away. Sam reasoned with Mama. He said that it was one less mouth to feed, and in return, they now had a reliable car to drive to work. "I ain't riding to work with your crazy boy," he said. What Sam thought was a great bargain was just another bad decision. The foreman had cheated Sam. He sold Sam a junk car. Sam quickly discovered that the car was badly rusted underneath, and like his old car, it too often wouldn't start. In fact, it was in worse condition than his first car. Sam and Mama had to push the car most mornings, and because they were constantly late for work, they both lost their jobs. Mama was able to quickly get more work housekeeping, but Sam was tired of working for a living. He wanted his money fast, and he and his friends decided to make their money by making moonshine. They found a spot in the woods and built their still and started selling. The money came rolling in for Sam and the Turner children. On some days when he and his friends were making their deliveries, Sam would have me and his children carry water from the spring to his still. He didn't mind me knowing the business because I was helping him, but he never bought or gave me anything. He would say to me at times, "You ain't my child." I was hurt when he bought his children presents and wouldn't give me anything. I felt as if I didn't belong there. The summer of 1948, Luther had found our papa in South Georgia and began visiting him often. When I found out my papa was in Georgia, I was anxious to visit him. He invited me, but Mama forbade me to go. She was scared that I would not come back. I wanted Sam to know that I had a papa, and maybe he would want to keep me for a while. I was ready to stay in Georgia. I needed some time away from Sam and his children. I was also hurt when I got the news that Molly's colt had gotten out of her fence at her new home and was hit by a train as she tried to cross the tracks. It was becoming harder by the day to live with Sam and all of his troubles, and he had a lot of them.

The police began to come down hard on moonshiners, and now Sam and his friends were finding it hard to sell their liquor. Sam would sell almost anything he could get his hands on. One day Mama came out of the house to see the town butcher taking her cow to slaughter. She shouted at him, asking the man what he was doing with her cow. The man stated that Sam had sold him the cow that morning. Later that evening the man returned to the house, looking for Sam. He was furious because the cow he had slaughtered was pregnant and the meat was ruined. The man insisted his money be returned, but by that time Sam was gone. Sam stayed away from home more and more since he had started selling his illegal liquor. He was always a few steps ahead of the law. Cheating an honest businessman was just another way for Sam to make his fast money. When Mama confronted Sam about selling her cow, he was full of anger, cussing.

"I done told you I don't want to talk about that cow. I needed the money, and that's all you need to know." Mama quickly stopped the conversation, not wanting to anger Sam any further. We never knew when Sam would be home. He usually would leave when he had money, and he would return when the money was gone. He usually returned home to see what he could sell for some quick cash. He spent more and more time away. He didn't have time for Mama or the children he once prized. Sam didn't think twice about any of us, he didn't care. When I turned fifteen, Mama was concerned because I was becoming even more withdrawn. I was only spending time with my younger sisters and brother and some of the elderly people in the neighborhood.

I loved being around the old folks, and I would listen to some of their stories. I was fascinated with what they had to say, and I loved how their gray hair would shine in the sun. I felt their stories were special treasures of wisdom. I learned a lot from them. I loved children and offered to babysit for some of the neighbors. I loved to hold newborn babies and sing to them. They were nothing like the Turner children. In fact, I had never seen children act like Sam's. Mama encouraged me to spend more time with my friends, and I was even allowed to work in the kitchen at a local restaurant. We needed the money. When the Turner children were school age, Sam insisted that Mama send his children to school. I wished he had encouraged her to send me to school too, but he never spoke a word to her about my education. I was socializing with my friends, and I was making money. I was helping Mama as much as I could since Sam wasn't around and there were expenses for the children. They always wanted something new, and they wanted it immediately. And they didn't have a problem with insisting that Mama produce whatever it was that they wanted.

Chapter 4

Another Season

Things were beginning to look better for me. Sam wasn't home most of the time, and I was going to the café in the evenings with my friends. My friends and I would sit around and talk and drink sodas and dance to the latest music. I had a job, and I was making money. I had met a nice young man named Bill, and soon another addition to the family was coming. Luther and his wife, Mabel, were expecting a baby, but they were beginning to tire of our town again. That spring Mabel delivered a healthy baby boy they named Robert. Luther and Mabel were young, and they were too busy having fun to take care of a baby. Mama was concerned about baby Robert not having a steady place to live, and she took Robert into our home. She wanted her first grandbaby home with her. The thought of constantly moving Robert worried Mama. Luther and Mabel were busy traveling, so it wasn't hard for them to let Robert come live with us. Robert was such a delight and a great addition to the family. I loved him as if he were my own. Mama and I gave him as much time and love that we could. There wasn't a day that went by Robert didn't feel that he was someone special to me. Sam wasn't happy with baby Robert being in the house. He reminded him of his father, Luther, and Sam hated Luther. Since Sam was rarely home, he didn't complain too much about the baby being around. As the Turner children grew, they became even more unbearable to live with. They complained and fought about everything. They were rude and very disrespectful to everyone, especially Mama. They were so used to having their way, and if Mama tried any kind of discipline, they would quickly inform Sam the minute he came home.

Now three years had passed, and Sam was still in and out of the house. But one day he came home he said to stay for good. By this time there were more changes in my life. I married Bill and moved to the next town. I was ready to get out of that house, but I was concerned for Mama and Robert, who was now three years old. Robert wasn't happy when I moved out. I wanted to take him with me, but Mama said no. I was busy setting up my own home, but as the years passed, I began to start my own family. I tried to visit Mama as much as I could. I learned to drive, and if Bill had the car, Luther would bring Mama over for the day, or he would take me to visit Mama. One day when I was visiting Mama, Robert starting crying when I was leaving, and he would not stop. He started putting dirt and rocks in his mouth. "Why did you leave me here? I want to go with you," he cried. He wanted to live with me, and he was angry because I had left him. I later found out why Robert did not want to live in that house. It was the Turner children. They were always being mean to Robert. Craig was the worst when it came to being cruel to Robert. He would push Robert to the ground, and Sam encouraged their bad behavior. Once before I married, Sam told Craig to push Robert down and then kick him. Mama and I watched Craig continue to kick and stomp Robert as he lay on the ground, crying in fear and pain. We just watched and cried as poor Robert lay on the ground, helpless. Sam had us all afraid to speak up, and I regret that Mama and I were not strong or brave enough to help Robert. "Knock him down and kick that son of a—" Sam shouted. Craig enjoyed beating on Robert, and Sam liked to instigate the fights. I guess that was his way of getting back at Luther.

Once after I left home, I witnessed Craig beating on Robert, and I told Craig, "If I ever see or hear of you hitting Robert again, I will make you sorry that you ever touched him."

Craig ran into the house and got Sam. "What's the problem?" Sam asked. "You quit making Craig beat on Robert?"

"I told Craig, and I'm telling you, Sam. Don't you ever put your hands on Robert again, or I'll tell Luther what you two been doing to his boy."

"Ahh," was all Sam said as he turned and went back into the house. Poor Robert and Mama had to live day in and out with that mean man and his children. Mama and Robert did not have the means, or they didn't know how to leave. They were just living day by day, trying not to make Sam and his children mad. They were prisoners in their home.

Chapter 5

Time for a Change

My family was still growing, and I had a new job and was making good money. I became determined to get Mama and Robert, who was now thirteen, out of that house with Sam. The Turner children were always in and out of some sort of trouble. They were in their late teens and early twenties and full of trouble in the neighborhood. Mama couldn't keep up with their coming and going in her house. They never discussed anything with her. They were even worse as teenagers. Craig was Mama's biggest worry. He was just like his father, Sam, but Craig always made good on his threats. Sam would back down or run away from a fight, but not Craig. Craig would at times go out of his way to start a fight, and he usually won. He didn't care who he hurt or the means he used to do it.

It was summer, and Craig had started a relationship with a married woman in the neighborhood. I believe she was using Craig to make her husband jealous, but even if Craig knew this, he wouldn't have cared. My half brother Craig was more than six feet tall, and he had a light complexion. He also had a quick and hot temper. He always felt he could do whatever he wanted to do, and Sam encouraged that attitude. Mama told me about it one Sunday when I came for a visit. As I watched my children playing in Mama's yard, I made her an offer. "Mama, me and Bill are doing good now. Let me help you get a house so you can get some peace." By then Mama was tired and fed up with Sam and all the trouble he and their children was bringing into her once peaceful home. The house Mama had been renting for years was beginning to show signs of serious wear and tear, and she did not have the energy to keep it up like she used to. Mama quickly took me up on the offer.

"I got some money hid," Mama said and smiled. "I have money to put toward a new place, and with your help, we can do this, Sarah." Mama was happy, and I could see a hint of peace in her soul. We had a plan, and for months I worked overtime at my job. Mama saved money everywhere she could. We were off to a good start until the day Craig lost his temper and it cost them both greatly. Craig's girlfriend's husband had heard about Craig's relationship with his wife. According to witnesses, the man simply asked Craig to leave his wife alone. They were at a house party, and Craig was acting as if he was the woman's husband. He ignored the fact that her husband was also at the party. I am sure this caused a great deal of embarrassment for the husband. The man made no threats. He just told Craig to go away. Craig was not one to be told to do anything, and an argument erupted. Craig ran home and stormed through the door and passed Mama with the shotgun. "What you doing with that gun, Craig?" Mama shouted. Craig didn't answer. Mama tried to stop him, but he pushed his way past her and began to run back to the party. The man did not have a chance to defend himself. Craig didn't say a word to him. He just shot him dead. Someone called the police, and Craig was taken to jail. Mama was very distraught, and she kept apologizing to the man's family. "I have to use the house money to get Craig a lawyer," was all Mama said to me. Sam was silent throughout the whole incident. He only said, "He had it coming to him for messing with Craig." Mama and Sam hurried to find a lawyer for Craig, but they did not do their research. When the trial came, the lawyer was gone with Mama's money. He did not show up to defend Craig. The judge sentenced Craig to nineteen years in the state prison. The judge stated that although both parties had lost their tempers, Craig had time between running home and returning to the house to calm down. So Craig's shooting of the man was considered premeditated.

I spent some of my Sunday afternoons driving Mama to the jail to visit Craig. It hurt me and Mama to see him there, but it hurt me more to see Mama hurting so bad. Another piece of her life had been destroyed. Months later as I was visiting Mama, she smiled and said, "Let's get back to getting that new house." I was glad to see Mama back in good spirits. A few years had passed, and Craig's sentence was reduced for good behavior. He had almost served his time, and Mama accepted that her son was wrong and had to pay for his crime. I worked more overtime, and Mama kept saving. Together, we had saved a large down payment. When Cilia and Cissy heard about the new house, they were quick to say that they were not living in a trailer. "We want a nice house to live in." Neither one of them offered to help put in for the house, but they gave their opinion about what they were not willing to live in. Sam and Mama were not getting along as usual, and Sam soon moved out of the house again. This time he went to live with one of Mama's friends. Mama had once again been betrayed by someone close to her. Mama was so trusting and easy when dealing with people, and often these people did not do her any good. This should not have been a shock to Mama. Throughout the years Sam dated a few of Mama's friends. Whether Mama knew it or not, she never said a word to me about it.

The day came when Craig returned home from prison. He was unchanged and unrepentant. He quickly picked up where he had left off. He was still getting into mischief and starting trouble too, and Mama was worrying again about her last three children. Mama was now also raising another grandbaby. Cilia and her young son were living in the house. There were rumors about Cissy stealing the neighborhood husbands, and Craig was always losing his temper about something big or small. Mama had to live in the same neighborhood with her estranged husband and once friend. I was overwhelmed by all that Mama was going through, and I was expecting my ninth child. Everything was normal throughout my pregnancy, and there were no complications with the delivery. The concern came when I was not allowed to see my baby. "There's nothing really wrong with the baby," was all the doctor would say. After a day without seeing my baby, I got out of bed and sneaked to the nursery. I saw her for the first time, and she looked as if she was suffering. I just stood at the window, looking at her and wondering what was wrong with my baby. We were allowed to go home, but two days later we had to rush Marie back to the hospital because she only whimpered and her breathing was irregular. She was a beautiful baby, but her lips were blue. My father-in-law rushed us to the hospital because Bill was at work. When Bill arrived at the hospital, I asked him to check on the baby. "Something is not right with the baby," I said. After much questioning, the doctor reluctantly said that my baby girl had a problem with her heart and that she needed a specialist. Bill went to fill out the paperwork to have her moved to another hospital. While he was filling out the paperwork, our baby passed away. She was only seven days old. I didn't go to my baby's burial. Mama felt I had been through enough, and I was still too weak. Bill, my in-laws, and my three oldest children buried Marie at a small funeral service. It was a hot overcast day with the threat of rain. It was a very sad day for me and my family. Some have asked me if I have any anger toward the doctor who ignored Marie's condition. My answer is no. There is no need to hold on to any hate. I believe her doctor could have done more. Mama helped with the children, and she nursed my heart back to health. After a few weeks, we were getting back to our normal routines. I had no time to mourn. I was a wife and a mother with a family to take care of, and Mama and I had a house to buy.

As always, my visits with Mama concerned me more and more. Most times no matter how hot or cold it was, Mama would keep her door open. She would sit in the doorway and hold her hands together. She always looked like she was worried about something. I figured she couldn't be worried about Sam because he had been out of the house for quite some time. Cilia and Cissy were always out and about, and Craig was living who knows where. I would always ask her, "What's wrong, Mama?"

She would always smile and say, "Mama's all right." I always knew something was bothering her, and I always wished I could have helped her. The house for Mama was necessary for a new beginning. As time went on, Mama began to wear down even more than before. Robert was now a young man, and he had moved out. Mama was home most of the time by herself. I tried to visit Mama almost every weekend, and she enjoyed seeing her grandchildren. Two years had passed, and we were still saving our money. Mama was still excited about her dream of a new house ... until I got that awful phone call. Mama had fallen sick, and she was in the hospital. When I arrived at the hospital, Mama was in an oxygen tent. I panicked and asked the nurses, "What's wrong with my mama?" Basically, Mama was tired, and her arteries were blocked. It was a slow recovery, and I visited her in the hospital as much as I could. We spent time talking about the old days and the new house. The last day I saw Mama alive, she was sitting up in bed, eating grapes. She looked rested, and she was in a good spirits.

The next day Luther called me to let me know that Mama had died. I was absolutely devastated. It had only been a year since I had buried my baby, and Mama was there for me. But I wasn't there for her when she left my life. I've always regretted that Mama didn't get her peaceful home. She tried to protect me as best as she knew how like a mama bird protects her young. With all the funeral arrangements, I had forgotten about the money Mama was saving for the house. I suspected that Craig had found the money because my cousins told me that Craig was spending a lot of money in town. They were still taking from Mama, even in death! It wasn't worth asking Craig about the missing money because he would have denied it. It was time to let Mama rest. Sam did not go to the funeral. He just remained quiet. What could he possibly say? The damage was done. Sam would become mellow through the years. Cilia and Cissy moved north, and Craig moved from town to town and continued to stay in trouble. With all of his children gone, Sam would visit me and my family. I had forgiven Sam and all he had put Mama and me through. It just wasn't worth the fight. It was forgotten, and he seemed to be okay with being a sometimes visiting granddaddy. My children called him Granddaddy Turner. A few years after Mama passed, I finally met my papa. He had spent some time in prison for killing his second wife. He was probably drunk when he pulled the trigger on her. He explained, "She done me wrong." Luther brought Papa to my home, and I saw he was stumbling drunk. "What you got for your ole daddy?" He asked.

I said to him in a cool voice, "Not a thing." He was never there, and during his first and only visit, he was still not there. He was an alcoholic crazy man. It wasn't worth the fight, so I forgave him and let it go. I never heard from him again, and he was only mentioned again when I heard of his death. Forgiving and letting go has proven to be a very good truth in my life.

Chapter 6

Forgiven

As the years passed, Sam's health began to decline. The years of living and drinking hard began to take its toll on him. Soon he had various doctors, and he had been admitted into the hospital several times. He could no longer drive himself, and he was losing weight. I would often take him to his doctor appointments, and I would have to help him into the car. He was very frail and weak, and I helped him as much as I could. I'm sure some people might ask, "Why show compassion for someone who had caused so much trouble and sadness in your life?" I simply say, "He was my mama's choice, and I would help anyone who needed it." Sam was not there for me, but I made sure I was there for him because he needed my help. I paid Sam's friends to stay with him at the hospital so that he wouldn't be alone. Sam never offered any apology for all he put me, Mama, Robert, and my brothers through. I helped him with no regrets. I arranged and paid for Sam's funeral. I made sure he was treated with respect and dignity at the end of his life. Sam was my stepdaddy. He needed someone to make sure all was well at the end. I am not angry at Mama for not giving me the education I so deeply wanted. I tried to learn when my children started school, but after sixteen-hour workdays, I was too tired to concentrate. Sometimes I think I am too old to learn, so I encourage my children to do their best in school. I will achieve through them what I was not allowed to do, and one day I will sit in school and learn to read and write as they do. They will all graduate. This my husband and I *will* achieve. One day I will have sat at nine high school graduations. This I know the Lord will bless me to see.

Robert still visits me, and he still looks at me as a little boy who loves his aunt. He always takes a special interest in what's going on with me and my own family. When it's Christmas, he is always looking for that perfect gift for his favorite aunt. I love Robert as my own child. Luther finally settled into his own house, but he and Mabel are no longer together. However, Robert visits his dad often. Charles finally settled in Texas and is doing well, working in his wife's family business. Charles stayed away for twenty years, but he did come home for a brief time after Mama passed away. He gave no reason for his long absence without any contact with Mama. Luther was upset with him, but I didn't ask him for an explanation. Mama worried about him all the time. She was always afraid that he was hurt or that he had died alone. It wasn't worth the fight. I forgave Charles and let it go. I watch over my children with a fierce protective eye without fear or apologies. Like a mama bird, my daughter teases me at times. She says, "My Mama Sarah Bird."

* * *

"Mama, I'm ready to eat!" I woke up suddenly, and there was my baby girl. She was ready to start her day. I smiled and eased myself out of bed. I looked at the clock, and I saw that I had been asleep for about three hours. The pain was gone. The Lord had answered my prayer. I was alive, and I felt refreshed. "Let's have some French toast and a fried egg," I suggested.

"Don't forget *Captain Kangaroo!*" my youngest screamed happily. I went into the kitchen and looked out of the window. It was a beautiful sunny day. I could see a large dust cloud rolling across the field. It was my father-in-law in the field on his tractor, plowing the land. Everything was back to normal. I looked down at my baby and said, "I'd better fix your granddaddy something cold to drink. He'll be stopping by for some iced tea or cold water soon."

Still Not Broken

Mama's somber whimpers disrupt the
dark night's cool cricket sounds
Daddy keeps yelling as I hear each slapping sound
I sit quietly, motionless as I know that
we are the next prey he seeks
The steps draw near as I hear the stiff
boards creek beneath his feet
Yet, I'm still not broken ...
Mama is quiet now as he enters our
domain, we dare not look at him as
He calls us all kinds of names—yet, I'm still not broken.
My mind and soul yearn to run to
mama's loving arms, but today
she rests eternally in God's loving
arms. The man I've known
as daddy, is not my father at all, he
is my mama's chosen one
His fate is now my call-yet I'm still not broken
I care for him day and night despite his contrary ways
I forgave him a long time ago
After he sent my mama to her early grave
Today, I'm still not broken

—Kenyatta "Baby Girl" Judd

About the Author

Eugenia G. Crenshaw is a graduate of Mercer University with a degree in social science. She is a firm believer of stories with a *message* that impact life for the better. She's also a strong believer in education, self-help, and continuing education through reading and application. She enjoys writing short stories designed for people who love to read but lack the time for long novels. She truly believes the Bible passage "My people are destroyed for lack of knowledge." Hosea 4:6

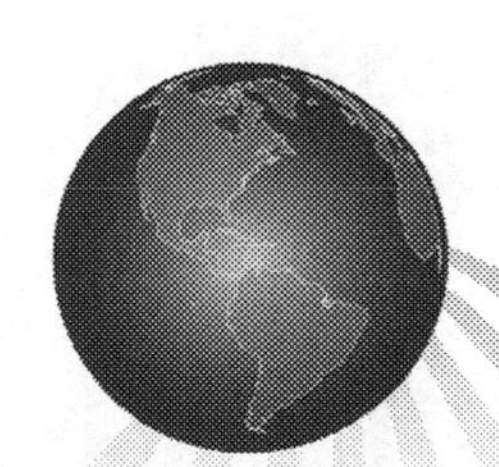

Eugenia Enterprises

Upholding all things by the word of his power

Printed in the United States
By Bookmasters